HURRICANE WOLF

Diane Paterson

Albert Whitman & Company, Morton Grove, Illinois

For Noah—D.P.

Thanks to Wayne Sallade, Director,
Charlotte County, Florida, Emergency Management and
Brian Mannion, Senior Advisor, National Science Foundation.

Library of Congress Cataloging-in-Publication Data

Paterson, Diane, 1946-
Hurricane Wolf / written and illustrated by Diane Paterson.
p. cm.
Summary: Noah learns about hurricanes as he helps his parents
prepare their home and while they sit out the storm.
ISBN-13: 978-0-8075-3438-0 (hardcover)
ISBN-10: 0-8075-3438-2 (hardcover)
[1. Hurricanes—Fiction.] I. Title.
PZ7.P2727Hur 2006 [E]—dc22 2005024608

Text and illustrations copyright © 2006 by Diane Paterson.
Published in 2006 by Albert Whitman & Company,
6340 Oakton Street, Morton Grove, Illinois 60053-2723.
Published simultaneously in Canada by Fitzhenry & Whiteside,
Markham, Ontario.

Printed in the United States.
10 9 8 7 6 5 4 3 2 1

For more information about Albert Whitman & Company,
please visit our web site at www.albertwhitman.com.

"**H**urricane Anna will arrive in our area by tomorrow morning," the reporter warned. "Winds will be seventy-four miles per hour or stronger. Dangerous flooding is possible. People living near the coast must evacuate. Everyone else should complete preparations now."

"My friend is lucky!" I said. "His family's going to the hurricane shelter at school. They'll get to camp in the cafeteria."

"Noah," Dad said. "It might be fun to sleep in the cafeteria, but this means they have to evacuate—leave their home—because it might be damaged."

"Our house is strong and far from water," said Mom. "We can stay home, but we have a lot more to do."

"I'll help," I said.

Outside, the neighbors were busy. Hammers pounded and saws screeched. Gray clouds raced across the sky.

Dad took the hurricane shutters out of the garage. Each one had a window's name.

"Hurricane Anna's like the big, bad wolf," I said. I painted a scary face on my bedroom shutter and wrote, "GO AWAY, HURRICANE WOLF!"

Dad said, "Nice work, Noah!"

We carried outside things inside. Mom took
the empty birdhouse out of the orange tree.

"Where do birds go when hurricanes come?" I asked.

"They know what to do. Some find safe spots nearby and some fly far away."

"I'm glad they're so smart," I said.

We shopped for extra food and supplies.
"Food that doesn't need to be cooked or refrigerated," said Mom.

"Just in case the wind blows down the power lines," Dad said. "Here's a flashlight for you."

We hurried home.
"Hurricane Anna is gaining strength,"
the car radio announced. A cardboard
box tumbled across the road.
Sheets of newspaper flapped in
the wind like birds.

We filled bottles and pails with water. We even filled the tub.

"Why?" I asked.

"For drinking, washing, and flushing," Dad said. "Just in case a pipe breaks and the city shuts the water off."

We put new batteries in flashlights and radios. We checked the first-aid kit. We put important papers in plastic containers to keep them dry.

"Just in case water gets in the house," said Mom.

"We're ready as ready can be!" Dad said. We plotted the hurricane's course on a chart. We tracked it on the computer. We watched it on TV.

That night, thunder and lightning shook the sky.
I made a tent with my sheets. I clicked my flashlight on
and off so Jake and Paddy wouldn't be afraid.

Storm shutters blocked the morning light.
"Power's out," said Mom. A battery-powered lantern glowed on the table.

The radio buzzed, "Anna, now a cat-two hurricane, is battering the coast."

"Cat-two hurricane? Two cats?" I asked.

"It doesn't mean kitty," Dad said. "Cat is short for category. Category five is strongest."

"I'm glad this is only a two-cat storm," I said.

Outside, those two cats screamed louder as they got closer. I covered my ears. Then Hurricane Wolf pounded at the door.

"Noah!" Dad said. "It's here!" He drew a circle on the chart.

I watched through a peephole. Trees bent and twisted. Rain shot sideways. A boot and nightgown flew by. The doghouse rolled over.

"Yikes!" I yelled.

Wind snapped and snarled. Branches scratched and clawed. The roof rattled.

"Go away, Hurricane Wolf!" I shouted.

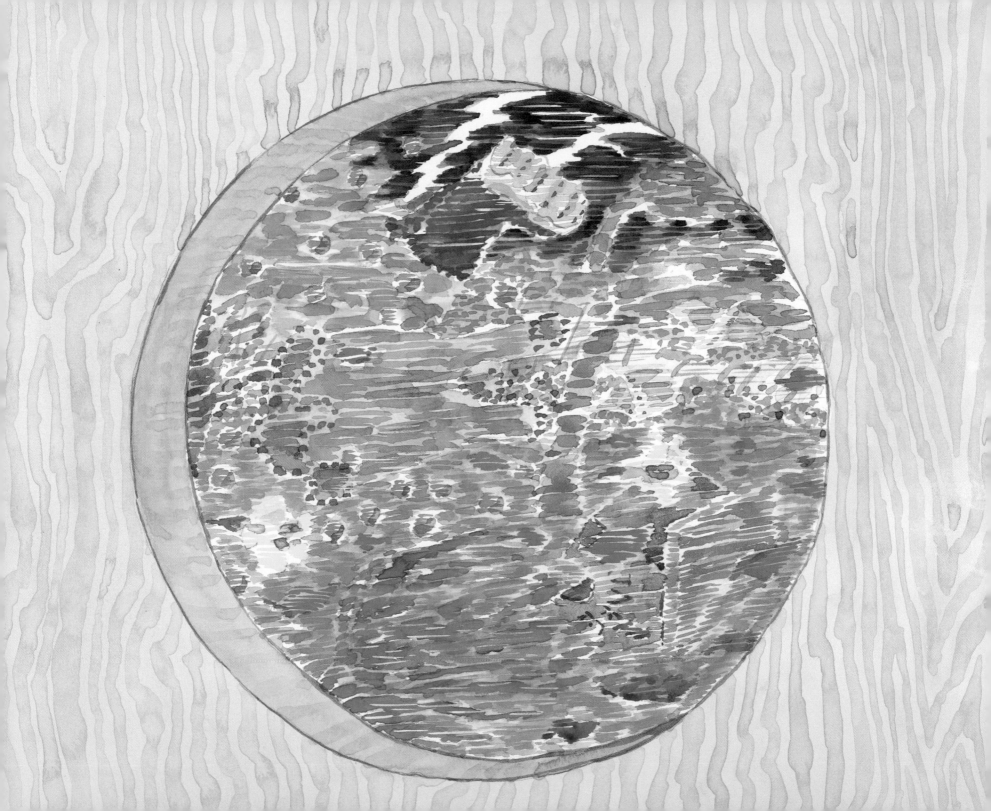

And after a while,
wind and rain stopped and
the sun came out.
"Wow, maybe I chased
it away!" I laughed.
"No, Noah," Dad said.
"The storm's not over yet."

"We must be in the hurricane's eye," said Mom.

"Can it see us?" I whispered.

"No," Mom said. She drew a picture of a hurricane. "This is the eye. It's the calm center that the storm whirls around. It's over us now. Soon we'll get to the other side."

"And the wind will blow the other way," said Dad.

He was right. The storm came back
again. Rain and wind hit the back of
the house instead of the front.
    I scribbled and scrawled.
I snipped and clipped.

"Who's afraid of Hurricane Wolf?" I asked.

"We are!" Mom and Dad said.

"Go away!" I growled. "You can huff and puff, but you can't blow our house down."

But still, it stormed all day and into the night.

In the morning, drumming and pounding stopped. Slashing and splashing ceased.

"Ah, good," Mom sighed.

"It's over at last," Dad said.

He opened the door and we looked out.

Everything was inside-out and upside-down.
"Wow!" I said. "This was only a two-cat storm?"
"Two really gigantic cats," said Dad.
Mom said, "I hope no one was hurt."

"Plants and trees will grow back," said Mom, "and we can fix everything else."

"I can help," I said.

"Yes," said Dad. "And you can be the hurricane chaser."

"Just in case," I said.

And I put the birdhouse back in the tree.

NOAH'S HURRICANE BOOK

Hurricane warning flags ←

Coast Guard stations used to fly flags to warn ships of storms at sea. Weather computers have replaced this system, but flags are still flown as a tradition.

Mom helped me make this book.

Me

Hurricanes

Hurricanes form over warm tropical oceans. In most years, about six hurricanes form in the Atlantic, but not all hit land. To be classified a hurricane, a storm must have wind speeds of seventy-four miles per hour or more.

Hurricanes are called cyclones in the Indian Ocean, typhoons in the Pacific Ocean, and willy-willies in Australia! The North Atlantic hurricane season is June to November. The Southern Hemisphere season is November to June. The Western Pacific season never ends!

Hurricanes rotate counterclockwise north of the equator and clockwise south of it. The storm rotates around a calm center called the eye that can be ten to twenty-five miles wide. The eye wall contains the strongest wind. Planes called hurricane hunters fly into the eye to test the storm's wind speed and direction.

Hurricanes can be two hundred to five hundred miles wide and ten miles high and move fifteen miles per hour. They can cause danger to people and great damage from winds, flooding, and storm surges. (A storm surge is a dome of high sea water that is pushed up onto the shore.)

If a news report issues a hurricane watch for your area, it means hurricane conditions could be present in thirty-six hours. When the news report says your area is under a hurricane warning, the hurricane will be expected in less than thirty-six hours. A hurricane watch means be prepared. A hurricane warning means take cover!

The Saffir-Simpson Scale measures hurricane strength by category (cat). Five is strongest.

Cat 1 -  wind 74-95 mph. Bad cat.

Cat 2 - wind 96-110 mph. Bad, bad.

Cat 3 - wind 111-130 mph. Awful.

Cat 4 - wind 131-155 mph. Horrible!

Cat 5 - wind 156 mph. or more. Most dangerous!

Fish swim deep. Birds fly away or find safe spots.

Paddy
Good cat

Each year, the National Hurricane Center gives hurricanes names - boy, girl, boy, girl.

Alberto

Beryl

eye wall,

hurricane hunter

Normal sea level

Storm surge

HURRICANE PLAN

If asked to evacuate:

Board windows and doors

Secure or move yard objects indoors

Turn off gas and water

Know a safe place to go out of the danger zone

Have pet supplies and a carrier, or arrange for
  boarding (most shelters don't take pets)

Fill your car's gas tank

Get extra cash

Put medications and important papers in
  waterproof containers

LEAVE EARLY!

*If you are not in an evacuation zone and
are staying home:*

Know the safest place in the house

Board windows

Move yard objects indoors

Have emergency phone numbers handy

Prepare a hurricane kit

HURRICANE KIT

Extra water

Nonperishable food for three to seven days

Manual can opener

Flashlights

Battery-operated radios

Extra batteries

First-aid kit and medicines

Pet food

Tools

Bleach and paper products

Bug spray

AFTER THE STORM

Stay away from power lines

Use phones for emergency only

Avoid flooded areas

Watch out for dangerous animals and insects

Avoid candles and flames

Use gas generators outside only

Watch out for nails and broken glass

Everyone cheers when the power people come!

Diane Paterson with Charley, rescued after Hurricane Charley and the model for Jake.

On Friday the thirteenth, 2004, Hurricane Charley's eye passed less than ten miles from Diane Paterson's house in Florida. "It was a four-cat storm!" she says. "Some of our friends lost everything. We were lucky. We only lost the roof off the woodpecker's house."

She hopes this book will help children understand hurricanes. "The more we know, the safer we will be," she says.

www.dianepaterson.com